The Tales of Grandpa Cat

Lee Wardlaw ✦ *pictures by* Ronald Searle

Dial Books New York

Published by Dial Books
A Division of Penguin Books USA Inc.
375 Hudson Street
New York, New York 10014

Typography by Amelia Lau Carling
Printed in Hong Kong
by South China Printing Company (1988) Limited
1 3 5 7 9 10 8 6 4 2

Library of Congress Cataloging in Publication Data
Wardlaw, Lee, 1955–
The tales of Grandpa Cat /
by Lee Wardlaw; pictures by Ronald Searle.
p.   cm.
Summary: When his grandchildren come to visit him
in his retirement community, Grandpa Cat entertains them
with exciting tales about the exploits of various
fellow residents—Billy the Kitten, Diamond Jim Kitty,
the Great Tabby Houdini, and Miss Kitty Hawk.
ISBN 0-8037-1511-0.—ISBN 0-8037-1512-9 (lib. bdg.)
[1. Cats—Fiction. 2. Grandparents—Fiction.] I. Title.
PZ7.W2174Tal 1994 [E]—dc20 92-39797 CIP AC

*The art for this book was created with ink, watercolors,
and colored pencil. It was then color-separated and
reproduced in blue, red, yellow, and black line.*

In memory of my grandfather John J. Laux,
who was never a cat but always told the tallest of tales
L.W.

A Sunday Visit

"Turn off the TV and get your sweaters!" Mom called. "It's time to go."

Christopher rolled onto his back. "Aw, do we have to?"

"Today is Sunday," Mom said. "We always visit Grandma and Grandpa on Sunday." Grandma and Grandpa Cat lived at Catnip Acres.

Ellen sniffed. "I don't like it there," she said. "It's boring."

"Yeah," whispered Fergie.

"No skateboards," Christopher said. "No video games."

"No shoe stores," said Ellen. "No beauty parlors."

"Everyone there is old," Christopher said. "Some of them don't have teeth. I'll bet some don't have tails!"

"Eww," said Ellen.

"Yeah," whispered Fergie.

Mom frowned. She tapped a paw. "Speaking of tails, I want yours in the car right now!"

"Yes, Mom."

At Catnip Acres Mom and Grandma talked and drank a cup of parakeet tea. Grandpa napped in his chair.

"Bor-ring," said Christopher. He stretched and yawned.

"Bor-ring," said Ellen. She polished her claws.

"Yeah," whispered Fergie. He stared at a dead spider.

Christopher sighed. He sighed so loudly that Grandpa woke up.

"Hello, hello!" said Grandpa. "Sunday already? Well, what shall we do today? Play checkers? Dominoes? Crazy Eights?"

"Can we watch TV?" Christopher asked.

"Let's go for a walk," said Grandpa. "We might find someone interesting to talk to."

"Then can we watch TV?" Christopher asked.

Grandpa stroked a whisker. "You betcha," he said.

Billy the Kitten

"There's someone interesting," said Grandpa. He nodded toward an old cat resting in the shade of a tree.

"He looks like a geezer," Christopher said.

"Geezer!" cried Grandpa. "Them's fightin' words to Billy the Kitten. In his day Billy was the Fastest Paw in the West!"

"Wow," said Christopher.

"Cool," said Ellen.

"Yeah," whispered Fergie.

"Billy could turn a rat into Swiss cheese faster than you can wink," said Grandpa. "When Billy strolled down the street, every rat would squeak and squeal and scramble to get out of town. Billy was the fastest paw for ten years. Until that Day. The Day of the showdown with Calico Jane."

"Who's Calico Jane?" Christopher asked.

"The meanest outlaw of all time!" said Grandpa. "Calico would rather spit in your milk than say hello. She used bad words. She never washed. And she robbed the Catanooga stagecoach every day at three o'clock. Everyone was scared of her. Everyone except Billy the Kitten.

"One day Billy went to Calico's hideout in the hills. He wanted to talk to her, eye to eye, whisker to whisker. 'Calico,' Billy said, 'you must stop your life of crime. If you don't, I will throw you in jail.'

"'Oh, yeah?' said Calico Jane. 'You and who else?'

"No one had ever talked to Billy like that before. 'That was a rude thing to say,' he told her. 'You should put your meanness to good use and help our town get rid of pesky rats.'

"Calico Jane laughed. She had a gold tooth that flashed in the sun. 'Catching a rat is kitten's play,' she said. 'I bet I can catch more rats in one day than you can.'

"'I bet you can't,' said Billy.

"'I'll make a deal with you,' said Calico. 'If you catch more rats than I do, you can take me to jail, lock me up, and throw away the key. If I catch more rats, you'll let me go free.'

"They shook paws. 'You're on!' Billy said. 'You have until sundown.' Then he raced into town, looking for rats," said Grandpa.

"He caught two in Mrs. Fluff's pantry. He caught four in Farmer Joe's barn. He caught six living in an old shoe at the town dump. By then it was sundown. He raced back to Calico's hideout. He was sure he had won.

"'How many did you catch?' he asked Calico Jane.

"'Thirteen!' she laughed, and her gold tooth flashed in the sun."

"You mean Billy the Kitten *lost*?" asked Christopher.

"Fair and square," said Grandpa.

"What did he do then?" Ellen asked.

"The only thing he could do," said Grandpa. "He married Calico Jane!"

"Eww," said Christopher.

"How romantic," said Ellen.

"They lived happily ever after," said Grandpa. "And had lots of adventures."

Christopher jumped up and down. "Can we talk to him?" he asked.

"Please?" begged Ellen.

"Yeah," whispered Fergie.

Grandpa Cat stroked a whisker. "You betcha," he said. "But wait—there's someone else you've got to meet."

Diamond Jim Kitty

A group of cats were playing shuffleboard under a striped canopy.

"See the gentleman with the gold cane?" Grandpa asked. "That's Diamond Jim Kitty, the richest cat in the world!"

"Ooh, and handsome too," said Ellen.

"I'll bet he has a TV," said Christopher.

"Yeah," whispered Fergie.

"Was Diamond Jim born rich?" Ellen asked.

"No, sir," said Grandpa. "Jim's family was poor. They lived in a dark alley. They slept on smelly rags. Jim's mother used to knit mittens and sell them on street corners to earn money for food. And they were always hungry."

"How did Diamond Jim get rich?" Christopher asked.

"Keep your tail on," said Grandpa. "See, Jim's friends dropped out of school. They joined street gangs. At night they roamed the alleys, picking fights. They sat on fences and screeched and scratched. But not Jim. He stayed in school, read lots of books, and studied hard. After school and on weekends he washed dishes in a diner."

"When did he watch TV?" Christopher asked.

"TV hadn't been invented yet," said Grandpa.

"Gross," said Christopher.

"Eww," said Ellen.

"Yeah," whispered Fergie.

"Jim worked hard for many years," said Grandpa. "When he got out of school, he had enough money to start a mitten factory. He hired his own family to work for him. They sold thousands of mittens. They made thousands of dollars. After a few years Jim was a millionaire. He became an aristocat! He bought a big house for his family in North Catolina. They had seven maids, seventeen cars—all Catillacs—and lots of fine, fancy clothes. They nibbled salmon and lapped fresh milk every day. Jim bought the old alley where he was born. He built a shiny skyscraper in its place. Life was grand for Diamond Jim! Until that terrible Day. The Day the stock market crashed."

"The what?" Christopher asked.

"The who?" asked Ellen.

"It's hard to explain," said Grandpa Cat. "But Jim lost all his money. He was so upset that he climbed to the top of his shiny skyscraper. He peeked over the edge. Then he took a deep breath and—jumped!"

"Ohmygoodness!" said Christopher.

"Ohmygosh!" said Ellen.

"Yeah," whispered Fergie. He covered his eyes.

"Did Jim die, Grandpa?" Christopher asked in a soft voice.

"Of course not!" Grandpa said. "He landed on his feet like any cat would! Then he brushed himself off and started over again with only a penny in his pocket."

"But how did he become the richest cat in the world?" asked Christopher.

"And why is he called Diamond Jim Kitty?" asked Ellen.

Christopher jumped up and down. "Can we talk to him?" he begged.

"Please?" said Ellen.

"Yeah," whispered Fergie.

Grandpa cat stroked a whisker. "You betcha," he said. "But first, look who I see over there in the garden!"

The Great Tabby Houdini

Grandpa pointed a paw at a silver cat picking plump tomatoes.

"What is she famous for?" Christopher asked. "Growing magic beans?"

"No," said Grandpa. "But she knows a thing or two about hocus-pocus. In her day she was called Tabby Houdini, the Great Magician!"

"Her hat is nice," said Ellen. "Could she pull a rabbit out of it?"

"Could she pull a TV out of it?" mumbled Christopher.

"The Great Tabby Houdini could do anything," said Grandpa. "With a wave of her paw she could pull a fish right out of your ear! Just as you were ready to take a bite, FLIP, FLIP, WHOOSH! The fish would vanish into thin air!"

"Wow," said Ellen.

"Cool," said Christopher.

"Yeah," whispered Fergie.

"The Great Tabby performed magic all over the world. Cathay! Catalina! The Catskills! Everywhere she went, crowds would ooh and aah. They clapped. They whistled. They cheered. They swooned. Yes sir, Tabby Houdini was the greatest magician in the world. Until that Day...."

"What day, Grandpa?" Christopher asked.

"Tell us, Grandpa," Ellen begged.

"Yeah," whispered Fergie.

"One day," Grandpa said, "Tabby got a letter written in gold. It was from the king of Catalonia. He wanted her to perform at his castle. 'If I'm going to do magic for a king,' said Tabby, 'I will need a new trick. A special trick. A trick that will knock their socks off!' Tabby snapped her claws. 'I know!' she cried at last. 'I will do a daring disappearing act!'

"And so she did.

"The king of Catalonia was excited about Tabby's visit. He had a special stage built for her. He ordered fresh cream for her dressing room. He hung balloons and streamers around the castle. When Tabby arrived, hundreds of cats lined the streets, hoping to see the great magician before the show.

"And what a show it was! Tabby dazzled the king and his royal court with every trick she knew. Then she wheeled a large purple box on stage.

"'For my final act,' said Tabby, 'I shall make someone disappear! Who will volunteer?'

"The king of Catalonia shouted, 'I will!'

"'No!' said his royal court.

"Tabby held up a paw. 'Have no fear,' she said. She opened the door of the box. She bowed to the king and said, 'Please step inside.' The king did. Tabby shut the door. Then she waved her magic wand and said, 'Catanooga-choo-choo!' BANG! Blue smoke shot out of the wand.

"Tabby opened the door. 'Ooh' and 'Aah,' said the royal court. The king of Catalonia had disappeared! Everyone cheered. Tabby bowed. 'Thank you! And now I will return your king to you. Catanooga-choo-choo!' she cried, and opened the door. But inside there was…NOTHING! The king had disappeared—every kit and caboodle of him. He was nowhere to be found."

"Where did he go?" asked Ellen.

"Did they ever find him?" Christopher asked.

"What happened to Tabby?" added Ellen. "Did they throw her in jail?"

Christopher jumped up and down. "Can we talk to her?" he begged.

"Please?" asked Ellen.

"Yeah," whispered Fergie.

Grandpa stroked a whisker. "You betcha," he said. "But first, there's someone extra-special I want you to meet."

"Who?" asked Christopher. But Grandpa was already hurrying down the path.

Miss Kitty Hawk

"Wait, Grandpa!" Ellen called. "Who is the extra-special someone you want us to meet?"

"Her name is Miss Kitty Hawk," said Grandpa with a twinkle in his eye.

"Is she a bird?" Christopher asked.

Grandpa laughed. "Oh, my, no! Miss Kitty is a cat, same as you and me. She has four furry paws, a stripey tail, and long, long whiskers that dance in the wind like wings. But from her very first mew, Miss Kitty wanted to fly."

"Why didn't she take flying lessons?" Christopher asked.

"Or hop a plane to Katmandu?" said Ellen.

"Yeah," whispered Fergie.

"This was a long time ago," Grandpa said. "Before anyone dreamed about flying machines. But that didn't stop Miss Kitty from dreaming. She used to lie in the soft fields of catnip on her papa's farm. She watched from sunup to sundown as birds streaked across the sky. She loved to watch them dip and swirl, swoop and glide. 'Someday,' she whispered. 'Someday, I will learn to fly!'"

"And she did, didn't she!" said Christopher.

"Keep your paws on," Grandpa said. "Who's telling this story? Anyway, over the years Miss Kitty drew plans on scrips and scraps of paper. Plans of a catplane that could take her higher than the birds, higher than the clouds. Then one cold, winter day, when she was just about to give up, something clicked in Miss Kitty's head. 'Jumpin' jackrabbits!' she shouted. 'I've got it!' She raced outside and set to work.

"All winter long Miss Kitty worked on that plane. She wouldn't let her family see it. But they could hear all sorts of strange noises coming from the barn. BANG-BANG. CLUNK. TING-TANG. CLANK."

"What happened next?" Christopher asked.

"On the first day of summer," Grandpa went on, "Miss Kitty's catplane was ready. She wheeled it out of the barn and into an open field. My, what a sight!

"Word of her flying machine spread.

"Everyone in Catville—even me—crowded around to watch and wait and wonder. Would she do it? Could she do it?

"'I'm off!' Miss Kitty cried at last. She gave the propeller a tug and a twirl. CLACK-CLACK! went the engine. CLACK-CLACK-VROOM! Miss Kitty hopped into the catpit and saluted the crowd. The plane rolled along. Faster and faster. The wheels were a blur. Faster and faster. The crowd held its breath. And then—she was up! Higher than the birds. Higher than the clouds.

"'I'm flying!' Miss Kitty sang. She swooped and soared, dipped and roared, and made loop-di-loops across the sky. Everyone whistled. Everyone cheered. 'That kitty flies like a hawk!' I said. And that's how she got her name."

"Wow," said Christopher.

"Cool," said Ellen.

"Yeah," whispered Fergie.

"But then," Grandpa said, "something horrible happened. A catastrophe! Miss Kitty's engine went SPUTT-SPUTT COUGH-SPUTT-COUGH. The cataplane plunged from the sky. The crowd screamed. Miss Kitty punched buttons. Twisted dials. Pounded levers. Nothing worked. The engine was dead! The plane went into a tailspin. 'She's going to crash!' the crowd said. They closed their eyes and cried. But then—at the last moment— Miss Kitty pulled up on the steering wheel. The nose lifted. And the plane glided right into my papa's barn, landing in the hayloft!

"I raced inside, leaping the steps two-by-two. 'Miss Kitty!' I called. Silence. 'Miss Kitty!'

"A pink nose appeared. Then long, long whiskers that danced like wings.

"'Miss Kitty Hawk!' I called. 'Are you all right?'

"'Purr-fectly,' she said. 'What fun! I think I'll try that again.'"

"And did she?" Christopher asked. He jumped up and down.

"Tell us, Grandpa!" said Ellen. "Did she?"

"Why don't you ask her yourselves," Grandpa said.

He opened a door the kittens had seen many times before.
They raced into the room and looked around. There sat a cat
with four furry paws, a stripey tail, and long, long whiskers that
danced like wings.

"Grandma?!" said Christopher.

"Grandma?!" said Ellen.

"Yeah!" whispered Fergie.

Time to Go Home

The kittens crowded around Grandma and held her paws.

"Is it true, Grandma?" Christopher asked.

"Grandpa just told us…" Ellen began.

"Christopher, Ellen, Fergie," Mom said, "you'll have to hear Grandma's story another time."

"But…" said Christopher.

"But…" said Ellen.

"No buts," Mom said. "Now, get your sweaters. It's time to go home."

Christopher rolled on his back. "Aw, do we have to?"

"Bor-ring," said Ellen.

"Bor-ring," said Christopher.

"Yeah," whispered Fergie.

Mom frowned and tapped a paw. "Give Grandpa a kiss and say good-bye."

"Good-bye," said Christopher. He kissed Grandpa on the cheek.

"Good-bye," said Ellen, kissing him on the other.

Fergie gave Grandpa a big hug. "See you next Sunday," he whispered.

Grandpa smiled and stroked a whisker. "You betcha," he said.